Don't Let The Bedbugs Bite 3.

Ooey

Gooey

And

Chewie.

By E. A. Green

BrEaKiNg RuLEs
publishing
www.breakingruleswritingcompetitions.com

Published By

Breaking Rules Publishing

Soft Cover – 10200
Published by Breaking Rules Publishing
Pompano Beach, Florida
www.breakingrulespublishing.com

Every illustration within this storybook book came from the internet's free domain.

"If Any Copyrighted Material Was Accidently Used," It was done Unintentionally by this Author and Illustrator Who Is More Than Willing to Remove Them at the Owners Request.

If things are getting stickily ickily,

You've slipped into the Greenman's

Latest Masterpiece of Nightmares and Horrors.

OOEY

GOOEY

AND

CHEWIE.

This Photo by Unknown Author is licensed under CC BY-NC-ND

The Clowns are Mad At Me for not giving them the proper recognition that they deserve.

So I, E.A. Green, dedicate this Masterpiece of Thrills, Chills and Kills

to those who whisper the dark stories to the Greenman's blackened soul.

QUOTES FROM THE GREENMAN.
EAKIE PEAKIE.

QUOTES FROM THE GREENMAN.
LOUSED LARRY.

QUOTES FROM THE GREENMAN.
CHEWIE LEWIE.

QUOTES FROM THE GREENMAN.
SLOBBY BOBBY.

QUOTES FROM THE GREENMAN.
BLANKETY BOO.

QUOTES FROM THE GREENMAN.
SCARAB GARRAB.

QUOTES FROM THE GREENMAN.
EWWGARI BOOGARI.

QUOTES FROM THE GREENMAN.
WINKIN, BLINKIN AND NOD.

QUOTES FROM THE GREENMAN.

.

QUOTES FROM THE GREENMAN.

If there are doubts about the right thing to do

Think how you'd feel if it was pressed upon you

And if you'd get mad or ticked from it all

Why do to another

That which would cause you to bawl

It's better to pick up your brother

And stand with them tall

Then to attack their character

Which can cause them to fall.

EAKIE PEAKIE.

You think your safe

Snug sound in your bed

And then comes the squeak

That causes much dread.

Eakie Peakie wants to eat

He's hungry to nibble

On stinky kids feet

You'll know he found you

By the bleeding bite sore

You should have stayed

In the bathtub more.

Hear his nails scrape

Across the house floor

As he searches for food

In your dirty bedroom.

Eakie Peakie wants to eat

He's hungry to nibble

On stinky kids feet

You'll know he found you

By the bleeding bite sore

You should have stayed

In the bathtub more.

The cookies smell good

That sandwich looks great

You shouldn't have snuck in

Your entire dinner plate.

Eakie Peakie wants to eat

He's hungry to nibble

On stinky kids feet

You'll know he found you

By the bleeding bite sore

You should have stayed

In the bathtub more.

Your hidden pillow candy

Says take a chance on me

Just sneak in the bed

After prayers are said.

Eakie Peakie wants to eat

He's hungry to nibble

On stinky kids feet

You'll know he found you

By the bleeding bite sore

You should have stayed

In the bathtub more.

Now bubble-gum lipstick

Is a fun thing to have

Until you wake up

With no lips to be had.

Eakie Peakie wants to eat

He's hungry to nibble

On stinky kids feet

You'll know he found you

By the bleeding bite sore

You should have stayed

In the bathtub more.

Now some people don't know

That rats love all food

Even the kind

That others abhor.

Eakie Peakie wants to eat

He's hungry to nibble

On stinky kids feet

You'll know he found you

By the bleeding bite sore

You should have stayed

In the bathtub more.

Is your nose kind of runny

Do you dribble while drool

Are there crumbs in your mouth

You're a smorgasbord fool.

Eakie Peakie wants to eat

He's hungry to nibble

On stinky kids feet

You'll know he found you

By the bleeding bite sore

You should have stayed

In the bathtub more.

So before you sleep tight

Brush those teeth well

And use only water

So your tongue doesn't smell.

Eakie Peakie wants to eat

He's hungry to nibble

On stinky kids feet

You'll know he found you

By the bleeding bite sore

You should have stayed

In the bathtub more.

And if you must snack

On hidden food stash

It's best to do it

In a room you don't crash.

Eakie Peakie wants to eat

He's hungry to nibble

On stinky kids feet

You'll know he found you

By the bleeding bite sore

You should have stayed

In the bathtub more.

Now before you sleep

The night away

Remember these

Keep Eakie at bay.

A cleaned-up room

A well washed bod

A Non smelly you

With a Winkin and Knod

QUOTES FROM THE GREENMAN.

If you hear a creeping

And a crawling after bed

TURN ON THE LIGHTS QUICK

You just might catch the monsters

At their favorite game

PICK-EM-UP-STICKS

They like to play it before using them

To pick

Poke

And prod

At their dinner

Before they eat on you.

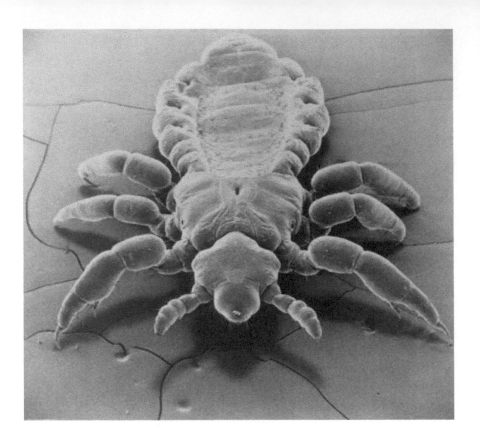

LOUSED LARRY.

Itchy

Scratchy

Bloody

Ewwwwww

Loused Larry

Is munching on you.

Six little legs

And teeth that bite

Claws that sink

And hold on tight.

Now Larry can't jump

Or fly around

He likes to travel

On things you've found.

Hair brushes

Hats

Scarfs and caps

Put them on

Or brush your hair

And Loused Larry

Will soon appear.

Six little legs

And teeth that bite

Claws that sink

And hold on tight.

You'd think he'd stay

In the home he's found

But he likes to travel

And get around.

You see his family

Grows real quick

One times two

Then hundreds on you

All biting

And sucking you dry

Digging for the brain

Before they die.

Six little legs

And teeth that bite

Claws that sink

And hold on tight.

Now the spider looking critter

Has no web to be found

But the sickly white dots

Say that he's around.

Your head will be itchy

Your skin will patch

As Loused Larry

Grooms his next batch.

And since the inn

Is now quite full

Onward to

Your friends must be

He wants to see

If they taste like thee.

Six little legs

And teeth that bite

Claws that sink

And hold on tight.

Now unbeknownst

To many sitters

In your bed

Is more of his critters.

Your pillow is

Home to many

And believe you this

There are plenty.

You see his family

Grows real quick

One times two

Then hundreds on you

All biting

And sucking you dry

Digging for the brain

Before they die.

So what are you

Supposed to do

To keep Loused Larry

From landing on you.

Wash your hair

Every day

And be careful

When you play

Keep others hats

Far at bay.

Don't brush your hair

With another's comb

And head scratching friends

Keep them away

Until someone says

Their safe to play.

All these things

You must do

Or Loused Larry

Will live on you.

Six little legs

And teeth that bite

Claws that sink

And hold on tight.

Itchy

Scratchy

Bloody

Ewwwwww

Loused Larry

Is munching on you.

QUOTES FROM THE GREENMAN.

If someone slings a mud pie of hateful distaste at you

DON'T

Be that person who calls in the public

To witness the issue you've now dressed up

Into a Three-Tiered Cake

It's better to just pull out your easy bake oven

And cook the offender

A piece offering brownie instead

Blow holes

Are much easier to plug

Than

Trying to keep one shut by retaliation.

CHEWIE LEWIE.

When it comes to chawing

Chomping

And a

Chew

Little roach Lewie

Has his sights set on you.

You can hear his mandibles munching

AGGRESIVELY

When he bites

As his salivary glands pool

While they sip

Drip

And drool.

Now the females aren't so bad

You can kill them with a swat

But Lewie is a boy

And that works

Almost not.

Underneath his exoskeleton

Lays a hidden vice

A set of wings

To fly away

So Always Swat Him Twice.

Another thing

To creep you out

His Six spindly legs

They itch

They scratch

And claw right back

To keep your hands at bay.

That is why

It's always best

To let him run away

But if you do

Remember this

You've now declared

A warring tryst.

Now Lewie is an eater

Of anything he can

From finger tips

To plump red lips

He even loves his spam.

And when it comes to darkness

Dankness

And night dew

If you've peed the bed

He'll always come for you.

You'd think this horror story

Would hopefully end right here

But unbeknownst to you

There's more than him to fear.

Two

Four

Six

Eight

Sixty-Four legs

And you're the bait date.

Twelve

Fourteen

Sixteen

Twenty

That count makes

More than one tummy

And you're so sounding

Deliciously yummy.

Thirty

Sixty

Ninety

AND MORE

His hungry family's knocking

On your alone bedroom door.

Now as you fall asleep

There's something you should know

They want to look you in the eye

Your lids are first to go.

Their angry and upset

You killed more than you should

So because of your hateful act

They've decided to strike right back.

No matter what the size

Or how long it takes to swallow

Cockroach bellies are never full

On your meat they'll wallow.

When it comes to chawing

Chomping

And a

Chew

Roach Lewie's family

Have Their sights set on You.

You can hear there mandibles munching

AGGRESIVELY

When They Bite

As their salivary glands pool

While they sip

Drip

And drool.

QUOTES FROM THE GREENMAN.

Did you know monsters have paparazzi

They like to take pictures of their shocked

And soon to be eaten prey

Why Do They Do This

They like to sell the pictures as Holiday Cards

During the Celebration of Krampus.

Your Photo is This Seasons

Most Sought After

Greeting card.

SLOBBY BOBBY.

When your feedin and drinkin

And hear a buzzing sound

You better cover that food

For Slobby Bobby's around

There are also other things

You should always do

Besides that protective feat

Before you bite and eat.

Clap your hands

And smash him quick

But if too slow

You'd best just go.

Buzz away

Little fly

Come near me

You're gonna die.

Now Bobby's gross

He eats whatever

Never ask him

Feed me dinner

He'll pick the trash

As stop number one

And number two poo

Will make you spew

It's big and brown

Sort of round

Runny too

No need to chew.

Buzz away

Little fly

Come near me

You're gonna die.

Now bobby's quick

And never slow

He dines in places

The living won't go

So hold your breath

Or you will spew

After you see

What's in his view

Its bloated fat

About to pop

Slimy green

And lots to slop.

Buzz away

Little fly

Come near me

You're gonna die.

Now for dessert

Your skins an oyster

Sweaty, unwashed

Smelly bad

And there's so much

To be had

He'll silently land

Throw-up a bit

Then suck your goo

Through his maw

While his tongue

Licks it all.

Buzz away

Little fly

Come near me

You're gonna die.

Now Bobby has

A few bad habits

He gets in places

He shouldn't inhabit

Your ear hole is

One place he likes

Your warm goo wax

Is honey times Max

And that opened mouth snore

Who could ask for more

A gluttonous Feast

On unbrushed teeth.

Buzz away

Little fly

Come near me

You're gonna die.

Now the sad thing is

You might just kill him

And proclaim you've won the war

But horrifyingly and defeating well

His Victory death rings a bell

It draws more like him in

So the best thing that

You can do

For peace and quiet now

Is go outside

And leave a Pooey

Of OOEY, GOOEY and CHEWIE.

Buzz away

Little fly

Come near me

You're gonna die.

QUOTES FROM THE GREENMAN.

Even if it goes against all advice

And Everything you now,

Never Be Afraid to do what Needs To Be Done

FOR YOU

"NO! MATTER! WHAT! ANYONE! ELSE! SAYS!"

Sometimes,

YOU

Have No Choice but to Change

YOUR LIFE

To Save

YOUR LIFE.

BLANKETY BOO.

Now, when it comes to urban legends; every civilization, every culture and every history book seems to tell, "and sometimes record," these far-fetched tales.

But, are they really that far-fetched?

Most of us have heard about Bloody Mary, The Hookman who stalked lovers lane, Slenderman and the one that, "To This Day," frightens every babysitter out there. Especially if it's their first time.

Mam, the prank calls are coming from inside your house.

Now, I'm going to share a True event that has been kept from the regular public and especially a specific kind of consumer that likes to shop at specialty stores which deal with those one of a kind, "and sometimes mass produced," items.

It's cursed retelling can only be found and heard around the campfires of those always on the move nomads.

Gypsy's.

This dying confession came from the lips of Lucia Kadilila, a pure, untouched and unmarried girl of nineteen. She shared it with her best friend Lavinia Codona before succumbing to the injuries that her boss Mr. Blackwell had beaten upon her after learning a Horrifying secret.

The baby blanket that Lucia had been order to hand craft, had been cursed before being bestowed as a christening gift for his, "now dead," new born son.

It all began the day he stood upon a table in the middle of the sewing room and announced to his workers that his newlywed wife was pregnant. Before he could be helped down, Mr. Blackwell just happened to notice a few things about Miss. Kadilila and her work area.

The dark-haired goddess was embroidering a baby blanket that he personally deemed A Work of Art.

He must have stood there a good Five Minutes, "watching her nibble fingers masterfully weave the most life like stork he has ever seen," before realizing that his trancelike gaze was now being met with one of her own.

And that's all it took.

She would be the chosen seamstress to create the One-Of-A-Kind blanket his child deserved.

She would also be the one who would end up being on the receiving end of his unwanted advances.

To make sure that his shenanigans didn't end up getting back to his wife and being the latest talk at the water cooler, Mr. Blackwell set Lucia up in a private office so that she could give her undivided attention to the specific qualifications that he was now requiring for this Monumental task.

His Baby was not going to be wrapped in a blanket produced by a machine.

Everything about his gift will be weaved and sewn by hand.

Now, "when it comes to Gypsy's," hand weaving amongst her nomadic people was a trait that was forcefully passed down from mother to daughter. If it hadn't been for that other tradition, "pre-arranged marriages," Lucia would still be traveling with the clan and not having to eke out a living working in a sweat shop in downtown Chicago.

There was no way she was going to marry the man her mother was indebted too.

Besides that, he was older than Methuselah.

As Lucia began her sequestered task out of the view of her fellow coworkers, she soon learned that being singled out by the boss is not always a good thing.

Between the jealousy, rumors and special attention he was giving her; she soon became an outcast amongst company. Even Mrs. Blackwell seemed to go out of her way so as not to have any kind of interaction with the seamstress.

As the young gypsy woman sat in her glass enclosed room, her question as to why she had been put in an office with a back door soon became apparent.

It was Mr. Blackwell's private way of visiting her so that he could grope and fawn over her without being seen. He had even tried to force himself upon Lucia once, but her knuckles forcefully cracking the glass for help, put an instant stop to that.

So, as the days turned into weeks, and the weeks into months; the Four by Six-foot blanket began to take shape.

And so did the deadly curse that was being whispered, weaved and stitched into every inch of its creation.

To keep her fingers nimble, "and making sure the curse would stick," Miss. Kadilila dipped her fingers into a mix of her own spit, blood and tears. She spoke sickness, heartache, death and insanity into every last fiber of that hand-woven blanket.

And the more Mr. Blackwell tried to take advantage of her kept away situation, the eviler those venomous curses became.

When the birthing day finally arrived, Lucia was just finishing up with the hand stitching patterns that Mrs. Blackwell Demanded on being a part of the blanket.

She wanted there to be at least One Hundred hearts embroidered upon the gift to their child. And after soaking the thread in over a pint of her own blood, Miss. Kadilila spoke a curse into every last stitch.

Death, Hatred, Insanity, Wasting, Heartache and anything else that a mistreated gypsy could think of as her heart began to harden and darken also.

It wasn't until Lucia's return to the threading line that the weight of Mr. Blackwell's abuse finally started to release its hold on her. She even began to smile a little more, when it was announced that the baby wasn't doing well.

With each and every passing day, the child became sicker and sicker.

As did Mr. Blackwell's wife.

She would wrap herself and the baby in the blanket and spend their days rocking each other to sleep as she cared for their sickly infant.

"During this time," her boss was so entirely caught up with what was taking place with his family, that his unwanted attention seemed to become something of a past nightmare which Lucia actually thought she could finally take a breath and move on from.

But, all that changed after his wife passed away about a week after their baby died.

He was looking for condolence and was going to use Lucia to get it, when he unexpectedly caught her in the midst of celebration and thanking her ancestral saints for answering her cursed prayers.

She was HONORING THEM with praises for fulfilling the

curses that were spit, spoken and weaved into the blanket. Lucia was also giving thanks for the unexpected gift that had been bestowed upon her also.

The death of the mother too.

Mr. Blackwell was SO ENRAGED, that he dragged Lucia into the room where she had woven the death shroud and proceeded to take out his anger, hatred and authority in a way some women's husbands tend to do after returning from the pub in a drunken and sexed up rage.

After taking her untouched purity, he left in a huff but soon returned in a puff.

Retrieving the blanket from his office, "where he had been keeping it as a soothing blanket to cry his misery in," Blackwell violently threw the death shroud at his new concubine and ordered her to destroy the thing the EXACT SAME WAY it had been created.

Stitch by hand sewn stitch.

The only instrument she would be allowed to use as she unstitched the blanket were her own teeth, fingers and nails.

And as the unwanted physical abuse progressed from one day to the next week and into the following month; that baby bedding became saturated with her Accursed Spittle, Venomous Blood and Broken Nailed Hatred.

Between her employers unwanted advances and the lack of proper tools, the unstitching and unweaving of the shroud took more than Six Months.

Approximately ONE HUNDRED and EIGHTY-THREE DAYS passed before those last pieces of thread were pulled apart. Laying at Lucia's feet were hundreds of feet of red thread that had once been whiter than pure, untouched snow.

And she had plans for every last inch of it.

Now that her boss no longer had a reason to keep her apart from the other coworkers, he no longer wished to look at the gal who was less than a ravaging beauty now.

He had destroyed her self-worth to the extreme that she quit caring about her looks, she stopped bathing and she refused to change out of her dirty work cloths. Lucia Kadilila was nothing more than an empty shell of herself that you could smell walking in the door before knowing she was even there.

Mr. Blackwell placed her at the far end of his factory warehouse so that he would never have to look at or smell her nastiness again.

She would be in charge of loading the thread spindles onto the machine that was used to spin the baby blankets that were being mass produced for the general public.

The haggard gypsy woman of Nineteen, "who now had the appearance of a Forty-Year-Old," gratefully thanked those that watched over her as she proceeded to use that which she had been ordered to destroy.

She cut the cursed thread from the baby blanket into Three Inch Strips and slipped one into every blanket the machine sewed.

There was approximately Eight Hundred Yards of thread used in the blanket for Blackwell's baby. That's somewhere in the distance of Two Thousand and Four Hundred Feet of yarn she now had to work with.

By cutting it into Three Inch Strips, Kadilila estimated that she now had the ability to curse almost EIGHT HUNDRED baby blankets.

"If it hadn't of been for two separate instances," Lucia would have fulfilled her quota.

The number of reported deaths of Sudden Infant Death Syndrome, "all sleeping with a baby blanket from HIS COMPANY," and his lust for her, put Lucia in the Bullseye of her Boss.

Unknown to Lucia, he had taken notice that she had finally started to care for her appearance and was starting to hunger for the feel of his naked skin pressed against hers once again. And the day he decided to do something about it, he unexpectedly walked up behind her just as she was placing one of the cursed threads.

Blackwell couldn't believe what he was seeing and hearing as she stitched that piece of thread into a Brand-New blanket.

As unto the Blackwell's, so unto you. Let the curse of a slow, painful and wasting death befall all those who purchase this and any others. That spoken curse was followed by a spit-soaked piece of thread being sewn into the garment.

She was the reason for his suffering.

She Was The Reason His Wife Died.

AND, SHE WAS THE REASON FOR HIS BABY DYING!

Out of the Two Hundred employees that worked the warehouse floor, every last one of them gave the exact same account of what was shouted over them all before he attacked Lucia.

I'M GOING TO KILL YOU!

And she would have died in his strangled hands if it had not been for her fellow workers and the best friend any girl could have, tearing him away from her crumpled body.

Instead of dying with Mr. Blackwell's hands around her throat, Lucia passed away in the arms of Lavinia Codona. The Only person who had any inkling of why this had just happened. She was also the only other girl who had suffered at Blackwell's unwanted advances too.

And like all good Gypsy's, a righteous curse is Never bragged about to strangers and those who are not of the traveling clans.

That's why, "if your one of the lucky ones," this story is only told around those darkened nights when someone is considering the same actions that Lucia had. Is there power, "still to this day," in her curse.

And the questionable answer is always the same.

Do you see a Blackwell's baby blanket anywhere in the vicinity.

Do you?

You will NEVER see such a thing amongst a Gypsy. Normal, everyday people are an entirely different ball game.

They Love his Baby Blankets.

I'm willing to bet that you might even have or had one yourself.

Even To This Day, Doctors are still unsure what causes SIDS in a baby. They have many theories but no answers to that unsolved question.

But Gypsy's Know.

They have Always Known.

If there is a Baby Blanket in the crib, "and it's a Blackwell's creation," the curse of Lucia has struck again.

So, if someone's baby unexpectedly passes away, was there a blanket in the crib.

If your young and always sickly; is there a blanket from Blackwell's in the room.

And, if others get sick and pass away around the same time as the baby did; were they wrapped in a blanket as they mourned.

If so, you Really Should check your own blanket.

"Because if it's from Blackwell's," Lucia's curse is coming for you.

As unto the Blackwell's,

So unto you.

Let the curse of a Slow,

Painful

And Wasting Death

Befall You

And All Those

Who purchase This

And any others.

QUOTES FROM THE GREENMAN.

Now some people sleep with their window wide opened

And others keep it tightly closed

But, Bugs can still get in no matter what

That's because they come in all shapes and sizes

So, no matter what you do

They're still going to get in and eat you

And as The Greenman Always says

Good night

Sleep tight

Because the bedbugs

Will always bite.

SCARAB GARRAB.

Beetles can be fun

And beetles can be stinky

But if you see a Scarab

Run away quickly.

These little beetles

Don't just spray and bite

They're a one-way ticket

To the afterlife.

The little dung beetle

Knows the day is short

It must lay its eggs

Inside a cohort.

Too bad there's not a body

Laying just around

Oh

Look

Here's one now

Upon you he has found.

Now you can turn about

And out sprint him fast

But once a Scarab sees you

Your soul he's set to task.

Now onward to

What must be

Answer His questions

To satisfy He.

To escape a Horrid Fate

For his eggs

Not incubate

These three questions

You must know

Or in your gullet

They all go.

Now onward to

What must be

Answer this question

To satisfy He

And

Choose your answer well

Or in your gullet

Garrab's eggs will dwell.

When we came to be

Was Khepri the God you see

Or amongst the brothers

Were there chosen others

Choose your answer well

Or in your gullet

Garrab's eggs will dwell.

Now onward to

What must be

Answer this question

To satisfy He.

The Middle Kingdom

Egypt saw

Did I rub

Their necks so raw

Try not

To hem and haw

Or you

Will lose it all

Choose your answer well

Or in your gullet

Garrab's eggs will dwell.

Now onward to

What must be

Answer this question

To satisfy He.

When the New Kingdom

Finally dawned

Did we sleep

Where Pharos fawned

Hurry up

And answer quick

Or Scarab's knife

Will lickety-slip

Choose your answer well

Or in your gullet

Garrab's eggs will dwell.

Now onward to

What must be

If you were lucky

And answered all three.

Is the sun still risen

Or gone away

This next answer

Decides your day

Choose your answer well

Or in your gullet

Garrab's eggs will dwell.

Now onward to

What must be

Answer that question

To satisfy He

For if the sun sat

And you didn't win

Into Hades

Your spirit grims

Full of eggs

Garrab's batch

And once they've fed

They'll meatily hatch.

Now onward to

What must be

Garrab isn't

Done with thee

There's one more thing

He needs to do

Before the last

Of you is through.

To be a Scarab

Of utmost high

It's now time

Your soul must die

So in the morning

He can rise

To pick another

For egg mother.

Now onward to

Who must be

Answer these questions

To satisfy He

And

Choose Your Answer Well

Or in Your Gullet

Garrab's eggs will dwell.

QUOTES FROM THE GREENMAN.

If people could say one thing about you

After your gone,

Let it be this

Every minute that life offered

You lived it to its fullest

You waisted Not One Drop

Of that precious gift

On nonsense

Self-hatred

Nor

The tearing down

Humiliation

Or destruction of others.

You Lived In Peace and Harmony with Any and Everyone

You were of ascension.

EWWGARI BOOGARI

Did you know

The quickest way

To losing all your friends

Snotty bubbles

Boogery Whoas

And always a finger

Up your nose.

Ewwgari Boogari

Kills that which it touches

Even a King

His Queen

And their Duchess.

Now we all know

This plague is vast

With no escapes

From its deadly blast.

Ewwgari Boogari

Kills that which it touches

Even a King

His Queen

And their Duchess.

A game of marbles

Can end real quick

When the slimy glass

Starts to stick

That is why

You should never pick

Or all your friends

Will end up sick.

Ewwgari Boogari

Kills that which it touches

Even a King

His Queen

And their Duchess.

Now as your nose

Turns bright red

The snot begins to thicken

And everyone knows

Your deadly now

And upon them your plague

they will sicken.

Ewwgari Boogari

Kills that which it touches

Even a King

His Queen

And their Duchess.

Now there's a way

To spread him quick

And make your friends

Extremely sick

Cough over there

Over here too

On all cleaned surfaces

You must Boogari spew.

Ewwgari Boogari

Kills that which it touches

Even a King

His Queen

And their Duchess.

As the petri dish

You carry inside

Multiplies and Sickens

All from you

We should run

Lickety split

And Quicken.

Ewwgari Boogari

Kills that which it touches

Even a King

His Queen

And their Duchess.

With boogers green

Chewy Brown Ew

And Sickly yellow

Very runny white too

Stop picking your nose

Like we're not here

With fingers deep

For a sweet treat

That you sniff

Lick

And then eat.

Ewwgari Boogari

Kills that which it touches

Even a King

His Queen

And their Duchess.

I share all this

In hopes to live

And for your benefit

Stop picking your nose

Eating your boogers

And running your friends away

For if you wish

For them to stay

Booger picking

Ends Today.

Ewwgari Boogari

Kills that which it touches

Even a king

His Queen

And their Duchess.

QUOTES FROM THE GREENMAN.

Did you know that parents are afraid of monsters too

For some reason, the little critters

ARE ALWAYS

Drawn to their bedroom when Mom and Dad are noisy.

That's why the parents of little monsters send

Winkin, Blinkin and Nod

TO YOUR ROOM

They know just what to do with little kids

Who Refuse to

GO TO SLEEP.

AND HERE THEY COME NOW!

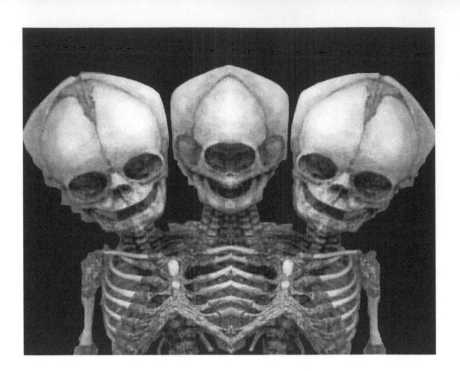

WINKIN, BLINKIN AND NOD.

Did you know

That there's a monster

For those who stay awake

He has two arms

And both legs too

But above the shoulder

Sits more than a few

And all three heads

Will come for you.

Winkin

Blinkin

And Nod

Know just what to do

If you refuse to bed

After your parents forcefully said.

There are things

That they need

And non-sleeping kids

Will fear their dread

As they give up

Their sweet little heads.

Winkin wants your eye lids

While Blinkin takes an eye

And Nod needs your neck

So tonight you're the pie

A slice of you they'll take

A piece here and there

But if you'd been asleep

All your parts You'd have keeped.

They hide in the corner

Or under your bed

Waiting to see

If you did

Exactly as

Your Parents said.

Will you lay down

Your sleepy head

Or stay wide awake

And play instead.

Winkin

Blinkin

And Nod

Know just what to do

If you refuse to bed

After your parents forcefully said.

Winkin wants your eye lids

While Blinkin takes an eye

And Nod needs your neck

So tonight you're the pie

A slice of you they'll take

A piece here and there

But if you'd been asleep

All your parts You'd have keeped.

Now as you nimbly play

Quieter than a mouse

They'll begin to move

And creep around the house.

Tiptoeing around

Touching things not

Leaving no clue

Of what happened to you.

And when you are found

That very next day

Your Horrified parents

Will have but one thing to say.

The last time I saw them

Was right before bed

I told them to sleep

Or I'd off their little head.

I didn't mean

The threat that I said

That's why I left it

To the monster instead.

I told them that

The brothers three

Will come get them

If they refuse to sleep

And then shared the story

Of that which creeps.

Did you know

That there's a monster

For those who stay awake

He has two arms

And both legs too

But above the shoulder

Sits more than a few

And all three heads

Will come for you.

Winkin

Blinkin

And Nod

Know just what to do

If you refuse to bed

After your parents forcefully said.

There are things

That they need

And non-sleeping kids

Will fear their dread

As they give up

Their sweet little heads.

Winkin wants your eye lids

While Blinkin takes an eye

And Nod needs your neck

So tonight you're the pie

A slice of you they'll take

A piece here and there

But if you'd been asleep

All your parts You'd have keeped.

They hide in the corner

Or under your bed

Waiting to see

If you did

Exactly as

Mommy said.

Will you lay down

Your sleepy head

Or stay wide awake

And play instead.

So when it comes

To beddy-bye time

Will you do

As your told

Or stay awake and play

Remember this

Before you do

A Three Headed Monster

Is Watching You.

And if you refuse

To follow through

And do as Daddy

Ordered you

Winkin

Blinkin

And Nod

Will Deadly Boo

Upon you too.

Winkin wants your eye lids

While Blinkin takes an eye

And Nod needs your neck

So tonight you're the pie

A slice of you they'll take

A piece here and there

But if you'd been asleep

All your parts You'd have keeped.

QUOTES FROM THE GREENMAN.

As you read this last page, please remember this

You are Unique, You are Fragile and Stronger than you think

Your feelings Do Matter and so does your opinion

Everything about you has Value

And you are worth more than Gold

And so is that person standing next to you

If you wish to be everything that you are

Respect those who walk this planet with you

Man or Woman; the poor, homeless, downtrodden, geek, nerd and

outcast,

Belong here just as much as you

Honor their value and they will honor yours.

If not, this world will never heal

It's time for ALL OF US to Cast Away Hate, Judgment and

Persecution

IT'S TIME FOR ALL OF US TO TRANSCEND AND LOVE

EACH OTHER

UNCONDITIONALLY.

CPSIA information can be obtained
at www.ICGtesting.com
Printed in the USA
LVHW010036250222
711932LV00003B/536